D T C

D1550027

This book belongs to

. . . .

. . . .

For Tim, who gave me the idea   D.B.

OXFORD
UNIVERSITY PRESS

Great Clarendon Street, Oxford OX2 6DP

Oxford is a registered trade mark of Oxford University Press
in the UK and in certain other countries

Text © David Bedford 2004
Illustrations © Emily Bolam 2004
The moral rights of the author and illustrator have been asserted

First published 2004

All rights reserved.
British Library Cataloguing in Publication Data available

ISBN 0-19-272554-8 PB

1 3 5 7 9 10 8 6 4 2

Typeset in Charlotte/Tempo Heavy
Printed in Singapore

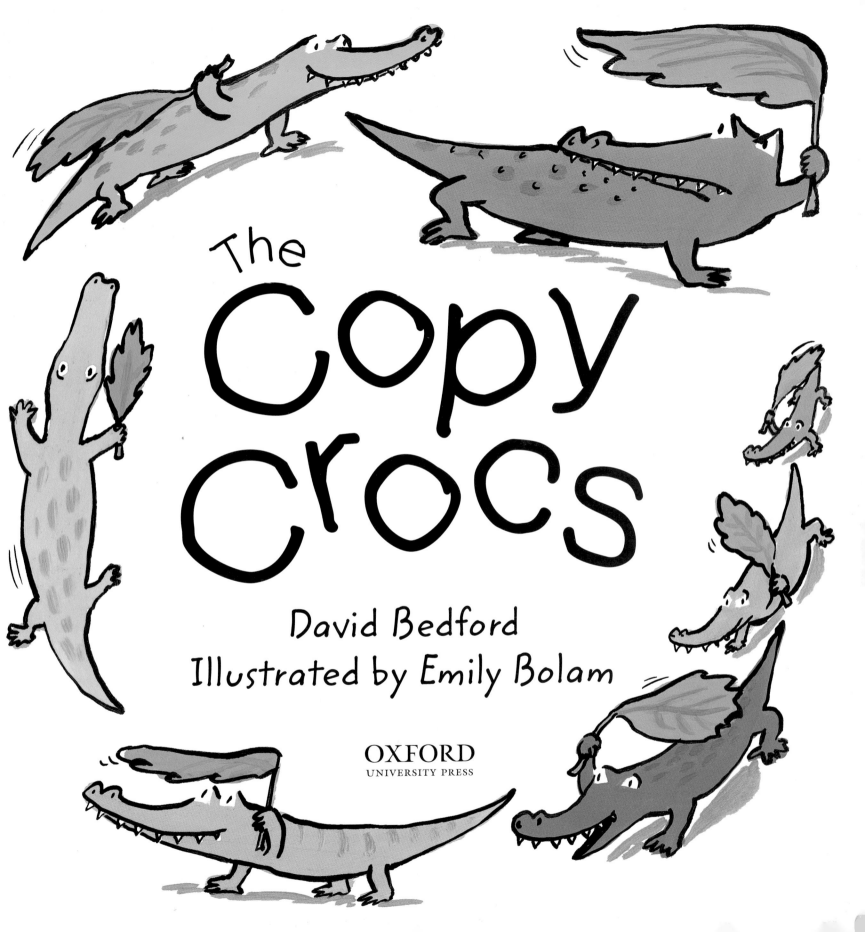

The Copy Crocs

David Bedford

Illustrated by Emily Bolam

OXFORD

UNIVERSITY PRESS

Crocodile had always lived
in the same pool, and he liked it.
But he **didn't** like sharing it with all the other crocs.
Every time Crocodile moved, he bashed into someone.
And when someone else moved, they bashed him back.

'Stop pushing!' Crocodile shouted.
'You stop pushing!' said the other crocs.
It was so crowded, Crocodile crawled out of his pool
and went to find somewhere else to live.

Crocodile's new pool was filled with slippery mud.

He liked it.

He really enjoyed sliding and rolling about.

But when the other crocs saw what Crocodile was doing …

… they started sliding and rolling too.
'Stop copying me!' shouted Crocodile.
But the crocs said, 'We can slip and slide if we want to.
It's not **your** pool.'
Crocodile was *so* angry he jumped out of his
muddy pool and ran away.

Crocodile found a place by the river
and stretched out in the sunshine.

He liked sunbathing.

But when he fell asleep …

... the other crocs came and sunbathed too!
Crocodile could hardly move. He was furious.
'Leave me alone!' he shouted.

Then he slipped into the cold river and swam away.

Crocodile found a floating log. He climbed on top,
kicked his feet, and glided down the river.
He liked watching the frogs and the birds in the trees.

And he liked being on his own.

But then he heard a splashing sound and …

… all the other crocs were floating on logs too!
Crocodile paddled faster.
When he passed a bend in the river, he hid behind some bushes.
The copy crocs were having such a good time they didn't see him.

Crocodile crept through the jungle until he
saw a mountain sitting all on its own.
'That's my kind of mountain!'
said Crocodile.

He started to climb it.

At the top of the mountain, there was only room
for one crocodile to sit.

Crocodile was happy.

But when the sun went down and it was getting dark ...

… all the other crocs squeezed together
on Crocodile's mountain too!
'Why do you keep copying me?'
Crocodile shouted.
'Because you're always
doing new, fun things,'
said the other crocs.
'Anyway, we can sit
here if we want.
It's not your
mountain.'

Crocodile
waited until
the other crocs
were sleeping. Then
he crept silently away …

… back to his pool.
Crocodile swam about everywhere,
and didn't bash into anyone.
He never knew his pool was so **big**.

But Crocodile felt cold and lonely in the empty pool.
He remembered how it used to be packed with a
snug pile of snoring crocs.

'I wish my friends were here,' said Crocodile sadly.

'SURPRISE!'

All the crocs were laughing, bashing and rolling about.
'Here we are!' they shouted.
Crocodile felt WONDERFUL.

He decided he **did** like sharing his pool
with the other crocs, even if
it was a bit of a squeeze.

But sometimes he liked to slip away ...

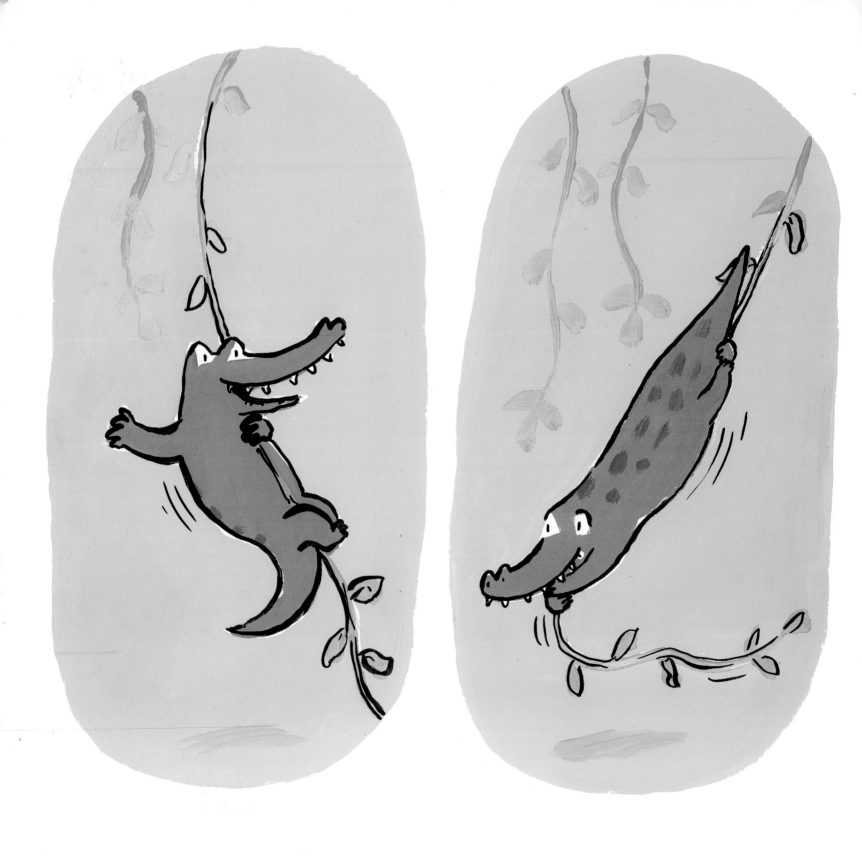

... *and do something* **on his own,** *before his friends found out ...*

... and joined in too!